JUSTIN'S ECSTASY

JUSTIN'S ECSTASY

Confessions

Book 3

LUKE JAMESON

Edited by

ANN ATTWOOD

Prologue

MATEO

I fell back on my narrow bed and allowed the tears to flow freely. The letter Justin left me fell from my hand to the floor, and a moment later I was curled up on my side, sobbing into the pillow.

"Why, damn it, why?" I cried. "This isn't fair."

There was a knock at the door, and I sat up straight and swiped at my eyes with the back of my hand. "Yes?"

"Mateo, are you okay?" An older man's voice asked. It could be any of the monks. I'd become such a recluse I couldn't recognize the voice.

"I'm fine." I lied, hoping whoever it was would go away.

"Pray, Mateo. God knows your pain, and can help you through it." The man mumbled, then I heard his footsteps walking away.

"Yeah, right," I muttered. "If God wanted me to remain a priest, he wouldn't have placed Justin on my path in the first place." I spotted the letter at my feet and scooped it up. Then I smoothed out the crumpled page on my thigh and read it again.

…I will never forget you or the times we've spent together. I decided to leave Holy Cross Abbey and move on to Richmond. This is my gift to you. After our encounter, you were crying, and I could see how conflicted you are about me and the priesthood. You said, "I can't go on like this, Justin."

"Damn it," I punched the mattress and a tear drop splashed on the paper in my hand. "At least I know where he went. Not that he'll want to see me."

If only Justin had known the real reason for my tears. I felt like Saul on the road to Damascus, but instead of a revelation from God, it was the sudden realization that there was no God. My faith was obliterated in Justin's arms, and there was no possible way I could remain a priest now.

I fell back on the bed and shut my eyes, then memories of our encounter at the gift shop danced behind my eyelids. Justin standing against the wall, and as I bit his shoulder my cock filled him completely. He'd cried out in pain first, but after a few strokes he was begging for more.

"Why does he have this effect on me?" I mumbled, then pressed down on my now erect cock. It throbbed underneath the zipper, and with trembling fingers I pulled it out and shoved my slacks down to my knees. "Because, I think I love him." I whispered, then fisted my girth hard and fast, anything to feel the same way I had just a few short hours ago. Images of Justin's face, his lips curled in ecstasy filled my mind. The memory of his tight ass wrapped around my cock made me moan.

"'I'm just a filthy priest," I muttered, and my hand flew up and down my cock faster. Pre-cum flowed down my shaft, and soon the air was filled with my grunts, and the slick sound of wet skin.

"You're no priest," I grunted through gritted teeth. Pressure filled my groin, and a moment later I gasped as cum covered my fist.

"Justin." I whimpered, then I raised my hand over my face and stared at the semen. Since I'd hit puberty, I'd always felt ashamed of my desires. The priests had told us it was a sin. Now? I brought my hand down to my lips, and licked it clean.

I ONLY HAD A SINGLE SUITCASE, and it lay open on the bed. My vestments and clerical clothes hung in the closet, where they would remain. I opened my drawers, and one by one packed the few clothes I had. It was only a couple of pairs of jeans, my underwear and a few t-shirts. Once I arrived in Richmond, I'd purchase the items I needed.

Fear and hope competed for space in my head. My entire adult life had been in service to the church, and now I was embarking on a new adventure. I'd do anything to have Justin with me. But, would he want to? Or was he still a hardcore believer, who would deny himself the love I knew he felt for me in order to serve a non-existent God?

Once my dresser drawers were empty, I shut the suitcase and pulled my phone out of my pocket. According to the website for the bus company, I had one hour before it departed Berryville for Charlottesville. Then I'd transfer to another bus which would take me to Richmond, a strange city I'd never been to. An AirBnB had been booked, a small studio apartment near the school Justin would be teaching at.

For my entire priestly career, I'd socked most of my pitiful salary into savings. Aside from a small amount I sent my family every month in Central America, I'd had no need for cash. What would I buy? Serving the church had been my life, and aside from purchasing the occasional book, money had meant little to me. Thanks to my frugality, I had more than enough to start my life over again. And if Justin wanted nothing to do with me, I'd move back to El Salvador.

A horn honked outside. I raced to the window at the same time my phone pinged. The Uber I'd ordered was waiting in the driveway. I picked up the suitcase and took a final look around my former cell.

"What an apt name, because it was almost a prison." I sighed, then placed the letter I'd written the Abbot on the dresser, and left.

* * *

DEAREST ABBOT,

Thank you for your hospitality over the years, but I've had a revelation. I'm no longer able to work as a priest, and if I try to hang on, it will end up being a disaster. I apologize for not letting you know in advance of my plans, but everything happened so suddenly. I wish all of the brothers peace, and goodwill. I'm not leaving any contact information because I'm officially leaving the church, and my reasons will remain my own.

Sincerely,
Mateo Ferdinand Castillo

Chapter One

JUSTIN

"...in the name of the Father, the Son, and the Holy Ghost, amen." I said, crossing myself. "You may be seated."

The boys in my biology class sat down, then stared expectantly at me. This was my first teaching post, and my heart was hammering in my chest. The students were in pale green military uniforms, and sporting crew cuts. There were only twenty-one kids, unlike public schools, which typically had over thirty students.

"My name is Father Finnegan." I introduced myself, and the boys giggled. Somebody must have tipped them off about my mother, or they'd seen Sister Angelica's show where Mom was drunk. No need to devote any time to that. "Open your books to the first section, on genetics."

I'd worried that the boys would be unruly with a new teacher, but they did as I instructed without a word. "Starting with you," I pointed at a young redhead in the front row. "Read two paragraphs aloud. Then the boy behind you will do the same, until we've completed reading the chapter. Take notes please, and sorry I don't know your names yet. I'll learn them quickly. What's your name?"

"Timothy Bankhead." The red-haired boy replied.

"Everyone, state your name before reading. Timothy, begin reading please." I instructed, then sat down behind my desk. The boy began to read, and my thoughts wandered. An experienced priest told me the trick of having students read aloud when you were not as prepared as you wanted to be. It took the focus off of yourself, and placed it squarely where it should be, on the students. It would also give me a chance to study the boys without making them self-conscious.

I'd gone to public schools in Los Angeles, and the behavior of these boys was markedly different from me and my old classmates. Everyone was paying attention and taking notes, unlike my former self. Throughout high school and the beginning of college, I'd been an excellent cheater. The lengths I would go to in order to not crack open a book were astounding. If I'd spent the same amount of time and energy on my school work as I did cheating, I would've been a vale-dictorian.

"Father Finnegan?" A boy's voice rang out, jarring me from my thoughts.

"Yes?"

"We were taught that Isaac Newton and other scientists were routinely condemned by the Church. What was the Church's stance on Mendel, the father of genetics?" The boy had olive skin, dark eyes, and angular features. Jesus, he looked like Mateo.

"What was your name again?" I stood, walked around my desk, and leaned against the front of it.

"Monolo Caro, sir." His curious eyes bored into mine, and I wrenched my gaze away from him.

"Gregor Mendel was a devoted Catholic. In fact, he was a monk and a teacher. Contrary to popular thinking, the Catholic church is passionate about education, and science in particular." I grinned at the class, and yet again, the boy named Monolo caught my eye. "Please, Mr. Caro. Continue reading for us. Everyone, take notes please because there will be a quiz on it at the end of the week."

AFTER CLASSES WERE over for the day I decided to walk across the city to see the Cathedral Of The Sacred Heart. The pictures I'd seen online were stunning, and since my small studio apartment was halfway between the school and the Cathedral, it would be an excellent way to learn more about my new home.

I also had another reason for going. The events at the monastery had provoked much soul searching, and I felt that going to confession would be good for my soul. The problem was, I didn't feel comfortable enough at Benedictine to unburden myself to someone who I would be working with every day. Even though what was said during confession was secret, people at heart were gossips. Sacred Heart was far enough away that I'd have at least a small measure of anonymity.

"There's no way I'm telling anyone I work with about Mateo," I muttered, then pushed the door of the school open and stepped out onto the sidewalk.

Richmond was a beautiful city, or at least the parts I'd seen so far. It was very different from California, much greener, though the air was quite muggy. St. Benedict's was in the museum district. Several enormous museums were within blocks of the school, and the stately old homes were stunning. It was obvious they'd been built decades ago, and unless they were split up into apartments, I didn't know how anyone could afford to heat or cool them.

"Father." An older woman crossed herself as I strolled past her. I nodded my head, smiled, and kept on walking. Perhaps I should stop at my apartment on the way and change into civilian clothes? Nah. If I did, there was a good chance I'd end up skipping confession, and watching mindless television instead. If I were to move on with my life, and serve the church, I needed to get Mateo out of my system. Confession was the first step, and then I could devote myself to serving the community.

"What the hell am I going to say?" I muttered, then realized I was crossing the street while the light was red. Several cars were flying in my direction, and I ran onto the grassy medium before getting run over. The street sign said I was crossing Arthur Ashe Boulevard. While waiting for the light to change, I noticed a beautiful Jewish Synagogue on the corner opposite me. Stained-glass windows covered the front, and like the other buildings around here, you could tell it was quite old, the total opposite of California, where everything was brand spanking new.

The light changed, and I finished crossing the street. According to my phone I was now in a neighborhood known as The Fan. Beautiful old row houses went on for block after block, then finally the spires of the cathedral came into view. It was on the other side of the local college, VCU. When I finally got to the entrance, I was struck by its old world charm. While not the largest cathedral I'd ever seen, it was lovely. It was constructed of smooth marble and stones, and when I strolled inside and glanced up, the copper dome nearly took my breath away.

A row of old, wooden confessionals lined the far wall. Before sitting inside one, I walked up the aisle and genuflected at the altar.

"I've never seen you before." A baritone voice startled me, and my hand flew to my chest. I turned and saw a slightly overweight priest with dark eyes and a beard. "Forgive me. My name is Manuel, but everyone calls me Father Manny." The priest stuck his hand out, and I briefly shook it.

"My name is Justin, and I'm new to Richmond. Just started teaching at Benedictine High School over in the…"

"Ah yes. One of the monks who runs the school told me they had a new teacher starting." The man grinned. He had an infectious smile, and I found myself relaxing. "Richmond's a small city, and most of the clerics know each other well. In a year or so it'll feel like home to you, I promise."

"I certainly hope so." My smile flattened. One of the reasons for coming to confession here was to retain a tiny bit of anonymity. Apparently, that wasn't to be the case if everyone knew everyone else.

"Is something the matter?" Manny locked his gaze with mine. "You look troubled."

Could I trust this man?

"Were you here to make a confession?" Father Manny lifted a bushy black eyebrow.

I nodded, and he gestured toward the empty pews.

"Actually, can we use the confessional booth?" I glanced around the cavernous sanctuary. "I feel a little exposed out here."

"Of course." The priest walked ahead of me and entered one of the booths, and I went in on the other side. I knelt and made the sign of the cross. "Bless me father for I have sinned. It's been a year since my last confession. These are my sins."

Father Manny said nothing, so I took a deep breath and began. "I have had doubts about my vocation." Wow. That just popped out of my mouth, and I hadn't even known I would say that. "I also had sexual relations with…" Shit. Should I tell him it was with another priest? Yes. "… a fellow priest while on retreat at a monastery. It's all so confusing."

"You are young, and I gather you only recently took your vows. Am I correct?" His voice rumbled through the elaborate wooden grill.

"Yes."

"Be more forgiving of yourself, because God is forgiving you. As priests we are to emulate God as much as possible, and that includes being easy on yourself." Father Manny sighed. "Almost every priest sins, Justin."

"But I want to be perfect." I placed my face in my hands and sighed.

"If you were perfect, you'd be God. He wants you to be at peace so you can minister to those in need. Now, is there anything else?"

"My mother." I shook my head, suddenly unable to go on. After a few seconds, Father Manny prompted me.

"What about your mother?"

"I'm embarrassed by her, and I know that's wrong. She went on the Catholic Channel, Sister Angelica's show to be exact. Then she…"

"Oh. Are you Margot Finnegan's son?" A note of curiosity, that seemed awfully out of place, tinted his voice. "I'm sorry, but she was just on a few days ago, and I saw the interview. I thought you looked familiar."

My cheeks reddened. "Yes. She was drunk, talking about me on national television."

Father Manny chuckled. "That's how you can tell she's a good catholic. She likes her drinks."

A little too much.

"I'm sorry, can we get back to what we were…"

"Of course, forgive me Justin." Father Manny cleared his voice. "What other sins do you want to confess?"

Why did it feel like this priest was enjoying my confession? Almost like I was a source for gossip. Suddenly, I didn't trust him, and decided to end things right now. "I'm truly sorry for all my sins."

"Justin, I want you to reflect on your life, and be more forgiving of yourself and others. Your mother is a catholic icon. I spent many hours watching her as Sister Marie Constance on Creating Hope. Nobody noticed she'd had too much to drink, that was only you." Father Manny's side of the confessional creaked. "For penance, say the rosary this evening before you sleep, and why don't you give your mother a phone call. Be a good son to her, because she's the only mother you'll ever have. Now, say the act of contrition."

Despite the words said, I didn't feel right. Almost like my confession meant nothing. "My God, I am sorry for my sins with all my heart. In choosing to do wrong and failing to do good, I have sinned against You whom I should love above all things. I firmly intend, with Your help, to do penance, to sin no more, and to avoid whatever leads me to sin. Our Savior Jesus Christ suffered and died for us. In his name, my God, have mercy."

Father Manny inhaled, then finished. "God, the Father of mercies, through the death and the resurrection of His Son has reconciled the world to Himself and sent the Holy Spirit among us for the forgiveness of sins; through the ministry of the Church may God give you pardon and peace, and I absolve you from your sins in the name of the Father, and of the Son and of the Holy Spirit."

I made the sign of the cross and murmured, "Amen."

Chapter Two

MATEO

The bus station in Richmond came into view almost immediately after we exited I-64. All the passengers got their belongings together, and a couple of minutes later, we were leaving the bus. After grabbing my suitcase from the compartment beneath the bus, I strolled into the station, hoping to snag a cup of coffee before calling a cab.

Almost every seat was taken, both in the restaurant and in the terminal itself. Despite the dozens of people milling about, it was very quiet, and most of the people appeared to want to be anywhere but here. I wheeled my suitcase outside and was about to call a cab when one parked next to me in the lot. I knocked on the window, and a moment later it rolled down.

"Need a ride?" An older man asked. I nodded, opened the back door, and sat down. After giving the man the address for the AirBnb, I sat back in the seat and exhaled. Though the monastery was in the same state, the entire trip had taken close to six hours, and I was exhausted.

"You new to the area?" The driver asked while turning out of the parking lot. He had bloodshot, brown eyes that stared at me from the rearview mirror.

"Yes." I yawned. "Not sure how long I'll be here for."

"You have a funny accent."

I could say the same for him. His southern drawl was barely understandable. Instead of answering, I grunted and shut my eyes. The man took the hint, and he flipped on the radio. It was one of those talk radio stations where everyone seemed to yell at the same time. The topic was immigration, and from the tone of the voices, they were very much against it.

Once the driver started talking back to the radio, I felt it was safe to open my eyes again. We were driving up a wide boulevard lined with restaurants and small businesses. We came to a stop at an intersection with a small circle of brown grass in the middle of it.

"That used to be where Stonewall Jackson's statue was located." The man pointed. "Damn woke fools made the city tear them all down. Monument Avenue used to be something, but now it looks like shit."

I recalled seeing news stories about tearing down the monuments. Personally, I thought it was an excellent idea. Who the hell wanted statues of racist losers lining what appeared to be a beautiful street? "Is Benedictine High School close by?" I asked, hoping to change the subject.

"Yes, sir. It's only a couple of blocks from where I'm taking you." The man turned down the horrible radio station.

"Would you mind driving past it? I'm visiting a friend who teaches there."

Five minutes later, we drove past a bunch of large brick

buildings surrounding an asphalt parking lot. Large stained-glass windows showed where the actual church was located. Nobody was around, and when I glanced at my phone, I noted the time. School had probably been closed for a couple of hours now, and I couldn't start my search for Justin if he wasn't there.

The driver made a right, then a left, and pulled up in front of a lovely brick row house with a big front porch painted white. A man was sitting on the top step, probably the AirBnb host.

"Need help with your bag, sir?" The driver asked. Since I was eager to be rid of him, I said no, paid the man, and got out of the car.

AFTER THE HOST gave me the key and showed me around the small apartment, he left. I'd booked it for six weeks, so after unpacking my suitcase, I decided to walk around the neighborhood before it got dark. Maybe I'd indulge myself and get a bottle of cheap wine from one of the many small shops I'd seen from the cab windows.

I'd also noticed several large museums on our way here, and wondered if any of them were still open. It was almost seven in the evening, so I had my doubts. But it was worth a shot.

The one that had caught my eye had beautiful grounds, and as I got closer to it I heard music. It was an enormous contemporary building, and kind of reminded me of Justin's mother's house back in California. Very sleek and modern. I followed my ears, and saw a small orchestra playing in a garden filled with statues and people dancing and drinking.

"Should I try to mix with these people?" I whispered to myself. Normally anxious in the presence of strangers, something drew me to them. Perhaps it was my new-found freedom? The last few days had been the start of an important journey in my life, and instead of shying away from contact, I decided to risk it.

The only way inside was through an entrance out front. There was a line of about ten or so people, and when I tried to walk through, a security guard stopped me.

"That will be ten dollars, sir." Her gaze traveled from my face, down to my feet, and back up again. I realized everyone in line had been better dressed and felt a little embarrassed, but I dug out my wallet and handed her the money, anyway.

"What's going on?" I asked. "I just arrived in Richmond and saw…"

"Every Friday night we have live music and cocktails. Helps bring people in." The uniformed woman replied absently. "Enjoy yourself, sir."

She handed me two tickets, which I assumed could be exchanged for drinks. There were maybe a hundred people milling around outside, all dressed better than me. Not that they were in suits and ties, it was that old-money look, very preppy.

I wandered over to the bar, hoping to get a glass of wine when I saw my worst nightmare: a priest in clerical clothes. He was about my height, but rounder. The man had dark hair and eyes, plus a closely shaved beard. If I could lay money on it, I'd say he was latino like me. My pulse ramped up for a moment, then relief washed through me.

I'm no longer a priest. Well, technically I always would be according to the church. The priesthood is like the mafia. Once you're in, you can't ever get out.

Since I was wearing jeans and a t-shirt, there was no way he'd know I'd just left the church. I knew for sure I didn't want to engage the man in conversation, so I'd just stay as far away from him as possible.

"What would you like to drink, sir?" A young woman wearing a tuxedo asked from the other side of the outdoor bar.

"White wine, please." I handed her one of the tickets. A moment later, with drink in hand, I headed to an enormous sculpture of what looked like the head of a baby. It was next to a gorgeous pond filled with water lilies and flowers. Nobody else was there, and it would give me a chance to take in my surroundings.

There was a marble bench next to the pond, so I sat down. The priest was directly opposite me, talking with a group of middle-aged women. The relief I felt earlier intensified. For the first time in years, no, decades, I felt free. No more doubts or worries about the state of my soul. For a moment, I felt pity for the priest, but who knew? Maybe he was a genuine believer, instead of one of those who bent the rules of the church thanks to ridiculous dogma.

I downed half of the wine, then swirled it around the glass absently. Though most of the priests I knew drank to excess, I'd never given in to that temptation. Even old Rafael, the priest I still loved back in El Salvador, loved nothing more than to tie one on at the local bar.

"I've never seen you at a museum function before." A baritone voice said from behind me, and I jumped in my seat. "Sorry," the man laughed. "I didn't mean to startle you."

I swiveled my head to see who it was, and my heart sank. It was the priest. Even without my clerical gear, it was like he could sniff me out of the crowd. "It's my first time."

"When it gets a little loud, I like to sit here and stare at the pond. Mind if I join you?" He asked. I bit my lip, then made room for him on the bench. He sat, then held his hand out. "My name is Manuel, but most people call me Father Manny."

Chapter Three

MATEO

"Nice to meet you," I mumbled, keeping my gaze on the little pond in front of us. Speckled Koi swam just beneath the surface, and I noticed a tiny green frog perched on a lily pad. Maybe the priest would take the hint and leave me alone if I ignored him.

He surprised me by asking in Spanish, "You have an accent. Do you speak Spanish?"

"Yes," I replied, then regretted it. I didn't want to give him any reason to talk to me. The man continued our conversation in Spanish.

"I'm from Peru. Where are you from?" He asked. I turned toward him, and a broad smile stretched across his chubby cheeks. Maybe he was one of the real priests who believed and practiced his faith?

"El Salvador. I only arrived in Richmond a few hours ago. While walking around the neighborhood, I heard music from the street and decided to check it out. This is a lovely museum." I felt my shoulders relax. I couldn't detect any malice in the man, and since he didn't know my past, he might be okay to talk to.

"The VMFA is one of the top ten art museums in the United States." The man said with pride. "I come here every Friday to enjoy the music, and of course," he held up his wine glass, "to catch a buzz. So, what brings you to Richmond?"

I opened my mouth to speak, and nothing came out. How could I tell this man about Justin?

Father Manny's eyes narrowed. "Ah, a man with a mystery. You don't have to say…"

"I'm looking for an old friend." I cut him off. Better to control the narrative, because in all likelihood, he either knew Justin, or would meet him soon. There couldn't be that many priests in this small city. It would be better to focus on him, not me. "So, unless you love cosplay, I'm assuming you are a priest."

"If I were into that sort of thing, I'd more likely dress up as a nun." Father Manny laughed, and in that instant I knew he preferred men. Another gay priest. Why were there so many of us, I mean, them? "I'm director of the VCU campus ministry. We operate out of the Cathedral of the Sacred Heart. You should come to Mass. The cathedral is like this museum, simply stunning."

That was the last place I wanted to go. "I'm sure it is, but, well, I'm no longer a practicing Catholic."

Father Manny eyed me, then drained half of his wine. My words settled uncomfortably between us, and he grinned, then drained the rest of the glass.

"Want to hear a joke?" He asked, and I nodded.

"A priest was driving home from a bar and got stopped for speeding. The police officer smelled booze on the priest's breath, then noticed an empty bottle of wine on the floorboard. He said, 'Father, have you been drinking?' The priest crossed his fingers, and lied, 'Only water.' The policeman shook his head, and said, 'Then why do I smell wine on your breath?' The priest raised his hands over his head and cried, 'Praise be to God! He's done it again!'"

I forced myself to laugh at the tired old joke, and Father Manny stood up and held out his hand. "Your glass is empty. Let me buy you another drink."

I hesitated for a moment, then allowed him to take it from my hand. "Thanks."

He strolled away, and I wondered why he wanted to hang out with me. I watched as he crossed over to the bar and noticed several older ladies greeting him. Father Manny obviously had a fan club, and I was a complete stranger. Wouldn't he…?

"That's it. How could I be so dense?" I murmured. The priest was attracted to me. I'd lay money on it. Throughout my career, numerous men of the cloth had put the jam on me. Since I'd walked around with rose-colored glasses on, I rarely noticed when it happened. It was only when they made an actual physical move that I'd figure it out. To this day, I'd only slept with one other priest, and that was Justin. But then again, maybe Father Manny was just being friendly?

"Here you go." Father Manny handed me the glass and settled on the bench next to me, his thigh touching mine. Was he boundary free, or did it mean more than that?

"Thank you." I scooted away. After this glass, I was calling it a day. Despite the beautiful surroundings, I wasn't in the mood to be around people, especially touchy-feely ones.

"This is a boring question, but what do you do for a

living?" Father Manny asked. I glanced in his direction and noticed him licking his lower lip.

"Currently, I'm unemployed." I sipped my wine. "But I used to be a teacher. Not sure what I want to do next."

"Oh, where did you teach?" The priest laid his hand on my thigh, and I froze. He stared at me a moment, then pulled it away and sighed.

"Um, you wouldn't know it. It was in California." Why did I have such a problem lying? I wanted nothing to do with this priest, and I'd say anything to get him to leave me alone.

"Father Manny, there you are!" A woman in her forties with bright red hair came running over. The priest's cheeks reddened, and he moved away from me. "You won't believe who I ran into." The woman said breathlessly, then her gaze settled on me. A smile spread across her face. "I'm sorry, am I interrupting something?"

I drained the rest of the wine and stood. "No, I was just leaving." The priest tilted his head down and frowned. "It was nice to meet you, Father Manny." The woman opened her mouth to speak, but I hurried away before getting dragged into a conversation with them.

After leaving the empty glass on a tray next to the bar, I nearly ran toward the exit. When I reached the sidewalk, I saw a bench at a bus stop and sat, trying to bring my breathing under control. When I'd left the monastery, the idea of running into a member of the clergy wasn't even a thought in my mind. Now that it had happened, confusion settled into my limbs.

"Why the anxiety?" I muttered, then put my face in my hands and sighed.

Cicadas began their nightly symphony, and I sat there trying to make sense of what was happening. Guilt, combined with relief, was what I felt. Leaving the brothers at the monastery the way I did was wrong. I should've had the decency to say goodbye, or given them time to find my replacement in the gift shop. Though they ran it without me for years. Hell, maybe they'd given me the work so I could figure out the way I felt about the world, and my place in it. Didn't matter now, since I would never return.

A young woman strolled over and leaned against the bus stop sign, so I got up and left, needing to be alone. So many questions raced through my mind, and I doubted many of them would be answered soon. Like, why were so many priests gay? And why on earth were we drawn to the priesthood in the first place?

"To avoid damnation." I murmured, then saw my Airbnb up ahead. Back when I was a true believer, I hid within the church, hoping a celibate life would allow me to be in God's good graces. Now, I didn't think God existed at all. All those years hiding behind the cross, and for what?

"Nothing." I climbed the steps of the building, pulling the keys from my pocket. "Not a goddamn thing."

Once I was inside the small apartment, I sat on the scruffy leather couch and wondered whether any good had come from my stint as a priest. All I could think of was meeting Justin, and even that episode had been tainted by both of our beliefs in the church. I recalled Justin's silly idea that sleeping with me, a priest, would prevent him from being gay.

"Jeez, what a silly head trip he played on himself." I stood and went to the kitchen, feeling woozy from drinking wine on an empty stomach. Halfway there, I froze in my tracks, my gut clenching.

"What if Justin still believes he's a doomed sinner?"

Chapter Four

JUSTIN

"I'm pleased to announce that the entire class passed the quiz." I grinned at the students. "Apparently, you find Mendel's work on genetics as fascinating as I do. Who'd like to volunteer to replicate his experiments with peas for our science fair?"

Three hands shot up.

"Mr. Blakely, meet with me after class tomorrow and we'll discuss the project. Class dismissed." The boys quietly gathered their belongings and exited the classroom. After they were gone, I spotted a couple of pieces of paper on the floor, and I picked them up and tossed them in the trash. The students at Benedictine had to be the most disciplined students I'd ever known. No one spoke unless spoken to first, and not a single boy failed to study or turn in their assignments.

"Unlike my younger self." I chuckled, recalling my cheating ways. Taping answers to water bottles and underneath the brim of my baseball caps were just two ways I'd cheated. Now that I was an adult, I realized I'd only cheated myself. But then again, if I hadn't been caught cheating, I'd never have met Mateo.

Aside from assisting Father Robert with mass on Sunday, I'd spent the entire weekend actively not thinking about Mateo. Keeping busy was the key, and I'd scrubbed my new apartment from top to bottom, gone running twice, and shopped for necessities. Since I'd never lived alone before, I had to buy all the little things we took for granted. Things like a shower curtain, soaps, and cooking gadgets. But try as I might, Mateo never left my mind.

Since I was on a very strict budget, I'd shopped at local thrift stores. While shopping, I swore I'd seen Mateo. It was embarrassing, because I'd run halfway across the store, and of course it wasn't him. In fact, the only resemblance had been the dark, wavy hair. The man gave me a strange look when I said Mateo's name, and my ears burned as I apologized, then left.

"Keep busy and don't give yourself time to think of him." I snapped shut the used leather briefcase I'd found at the Fan Thrift store, and glanced around the classroom to make sure everything was in its place. Aside from a semester as a student teacher, this was my first teaching assignment, and I was determined to do a good job.

"Looks fine." I muttered, then flipped the light switch and locked the classroom. "Time to hit the gym."

ONE OF THE civilian teachers who wasn't a priest gave me the heads up about using the school gym.

Don't.

According to Bill, a French instructor, the students

wouldn't leave you alone while you worked out. So, I'd taken his advice and gotten a membership at the YMCA on Franklin Street downtown. It was halfway between my tiny apartment and school, so first I went home and changed into running gear, then I strapped on a backpack filled with towels and a change of clothes, and jogged to the gym.

It was a gorgeous September afternoon, though a bit too hot for my taste. Fall hadn't arrived yet, and the tail-end of summer was turning into a scorcher. Another thing I hadn't banked on was the stench of Ginkgo tree seeds littering Monument Avenue. The trees were beautiful, with bright yellow leaves. But the seeds that gathered on the ground beneath them smelled awful. It was hard to run past them without breathing in the stench.

The other difficult issue was ignoring half-naked male runners sprinting up and down the avenue. Most of them were clad only in skimpy running shorts and shoes, and I struggled to keep my eyes off of them. Several of them eyed me when I passed them, and I wondered if I'd stumbled upon a cruising ground for gay guys. If so, I'd better run a different route.

The YMCA was in a four-story brick building built in the 19th century. After checking in at the front desk, I strolled into the men's locker room and locked my bag in a locker. All I wanted to do was sweat, so I got on a treadmill to run until my body couldn't take it anymore.

Nobody was using the machines, so I plugged my ear buds into my phone, put on some generic dance music, and ran. The treadmills were in front of a large window facing Franklin Street, and the street was clogged with cars. It was just after 5 p.m., and the downtown office buildings were emptying. Occasionally a jogger would cross my eyeline, but mostly I kept my mind blank.

Until a man who looked exactly like Mateo strolled by on the sidewalk. I froze, then nearly fell off the treadmill since I'd stopped and it hadn't. My first instinct was to run outside and catch the man. But I recalled the stranger I'd almost accosted in the thrift store over the weekend, and knew it couldn't be Mateo. I was imagining stuff, and missing him, yet I knew I'd done the right thing leaving him at the monastery.

"Damn it." I muttered, then increased my running speed. Sweat poured off me while I tried to make my brain blank out. Thinking of Mateo was counter-productive. Both of us were priests who'd vowed to God we'd remain celibate. Plus, Mateo was hours away in the mountains. It's not like he'd chase me here to Richmond. "But what if he did?"

Shit. I needed to derail this line of thinking, because nothing good would come of it. All it would do was trigger memories of Mateo, of being in his arms again. My eyes stung from either tears, sweat, or a combination of them both. At the monastery, I'd seen Mateo's simple life, and how happy he was.

Until I'd ruined it.

That's all I was capable of. Ruining his simple, pious life. When we first met four years ago in California, his happiness was overpowering. Goodness radiated from him, and his joy of teaching could be felt as he excitedly lectured his students. But then I had to ruin everything with my insane delusions.

"Hah!" I barked out a laugh and felt a pain in my upper thigh. I adjusted the machine to a lower level and kept running. How did I trick myself into thinking Mateo could somehow make me not gay? I mean, the definition of a gay man was someone attracted to his own sex, and fucking Mateo wasn't going to suddenly make me prefer women. But I'd wrapped my head around that delusion, and in the process, chased Mateo away. Chased him from his true vocation as a teacher and a priest.

I was a selfish man who'd known Mateo might be at Holy Cross Abbey. No matter how much I tried to deny it, I'd stalked him to the monastery. Then I'd taken advantage of him and ruined his peaceful existence. I'd apologized in the note I'd left him, but that wasn't enough. Now, I had to stay away from him forever, and maybe, just maybe, he'd find peace within the church again.

"Damn it." I hit the stop button and clutched my thigh. There was no way I'd be able to walk home, much less run it. I wiped my face off with the towel I'd brought, then tossed it around my shoulders and limped back to the locker room. My mother had a sauna attached to the swimming pool back home, and I knew they also had one here. Hot steam was exactly what I needed. Maybe baking the sinful thoughts out of my head would keep my demons at bay.

THE SAUNA SMELLED LIKE BLEACH, which was a good thing, though my sinuses stung when I first walked in. There was only one other man in it, and I sat across from him and shut my eyes. Of course, the first thing I thought about was Mateo. And since I was only wearing a towel, I immediately forced myself to think of the nuns who'd taught me in school. Anything to keep my dick from misbehaving.

"Is that you, Justin?" I heard footsteps approach and

opened my eyes as a man sat next to me. "It's me, Father Manny."

"Oh, hi." I sighed, then crossed my arms over my chest. There was something I didn't trust about this priest. After hearing my confession, he should know I didn't want to be approached while nearly naked in a sauna. Like, give me some space. Instead, his wide thigh sat less than an inch from mine.

"Why are you at the Y?" He asked. "Isn't the gym at Benedictine more convenient?"

"Well, I want a life away from my job. Plus, they offer a discount for members of the clergy." Damn it. I wasn't in the mood to talk.

"Oh. I thought maybe you'd heard about… never mind." Father Manny shrugged his shoulders, then I felt his leg against mine. Good God, did the man have no boundaries? I was torn between stalking out of the sauna, or ignoring it. The thing was, I didn't have any friends in Richmond, and angering a fellow priest wasn't a good idea.

"Heard about what?" I asked. Father Manny turned his head and grinned a toothy smile.

"You know, about the Y. What goes on in the steam room stays in the steam room, if you know what I mean." He winked, and my gut churned. A second later, his hand squeezed my thigh, and I grabbed onto my towel to make sure it stayed on.

"Father, what are you doing?" I knew exactly what he was up to, and I wanted no part of it. But again, pissing off someone who was practically a coworker, and who worked for the Bishop of the diocese, wasn't a brilliant idea. I scooted over a couple of inches, and his smile flattened.

"What's the big deal, Justin? It's just a little harmless fun between us guys." He stretched his arms over his head, and then one of them landed behind my shoulders. "Everyone does it. Like, I've fooled around with lots of priests who don't make it into such a drama."

I stood up and glared at him. "After hearing my confession, and knowing the hell I've gone through because of the awful decisions I've made, you actually believe I want to have sex with you?"

Chapter Five

MATEO

"If I don't at least try, then I might as well pack my suitcase and return to El Salvador." I punched the pillow next to me on the bed. Though coming to Richmond was a spur of the moment decision, I'd barely done a thing since I arrived.

Friday night after I left the museum I'd come back to the apartment and climbed into bed. Fourteen hours later, I woke up. It had been the best sleep of my life, and I hadn't known how exhausted I was. Since I didn't have a clue where to find Justin, I'd mostly wandered the neighborhood, taking in the beautiful architecture.

When Monday morning arrived, fear struck me. What if Justin didn't want to see me? Or worse, he was angry about our last encounter at the monastery. So, instead of walking the few blocks to the school I knew he taught at, I stayed in bed, only venturing out for the bathroom and ice cream.

But now it was Tuesday, and I realized if I didn't at least try to make contact with Justin, I'd forever be doomed with the what if syndrome. What if I found him, and instead of hating me, he fell into my arms? What if Justin patiently explained he was perfectly happy being a priest, and I could lick my wounds and eventually get on with my life? The list of what if scenarios were too numerous to count, but I needed to know where Justin stood in regards to him and me. I refused to move on until I had some answers.

Today, I was officially becoming a stalker. The school he taught at was a five minute walk from here, and hopefully I'd run into him. Of course, knowing my luck, school security would think I was stalking one of the students, but even if that happened, I could ask them about Justin, and hopefully he'd hear about it and want to see me. The problem was, I didn't know if he would. Again, another what if.

The note Justin left me was crumpled up on the mattress, so I smoothed it out and read it for what had to be the hundredth time.

… I decided to leave Holy Cross Abbey and move on to Richmond. This is my gift to you. After our encounter, you were crying, and I could see how conflicted you are about me and the priesthood. You said, "I can't go on like this, Justin." You're right, you can't, and my presence only distracts you from your calling as a priest. One day soon, I'll write to you in more detail about how I came to this decision. Until then, know that I have undying affection for you, and you will always be in my thoughts.

At least he didn't sound bitter, or angry. Justin had claimed undying affection for me, but would I ruin it by showing up at his job? Entire movies had been filmed about crazy stalkers, and I didn't want Justin to think I was one of them. But I had no way to get in contact with him. No phone number, personal address, though I guessed I could write to him care of the school. However, that came with substantial risk. What if the letter fell into the wrong hands and caused Justin trouble? He'd hate me forever if that happened.

So, I guessed I was stuck being a stalker. Now if I could only force myself out of this damned bed.

—————

COLD SWEAT DRIPPED down my sides as I locked the apartment door behind me. It took almost two hours to get up the courage to leave. Before that, I'd paced the small apartment, allowing every bad thing that might happen to race through my mind. Finally, I'd just grabbed the keys off the kitchen counter and forced myself to leave.

It was bright and sunny outside, the exact opposite of my disposition. The air glowed a faint green from the stunning trees overhead, the sun streaming through the thick canopy. Despite the beauty, all I felt was fear. But if I wanted to live my new life without regret, I had to see where I stood with Justin.

I heard the sound of children playing, and followed the noise. A few blocks from the school Justin taught at was another one, and obviously a parochial school. Little ladies wearing plaid kilts and starched white shirts played on a small playground, and the boys wore dark slacks and rep ties. According to a wooden sign out front the name of the school was St. Benedicts. Most likely they were being groomed for a catholic high school like the one Justin taught at. A nun strolled across the playground and scowled, and a wave of dizziness shot through me. Her gaze was squarely on me.

"Now I really do look like a stalker." I muttered, forcing myself to turn and walk away. Nuns were the scariest people on earth, and I wasn't about to tangle with one now. When I turned the corner, I heard a man's voice bellowing close by, followed by a group of men yelling back. Intrigued, or rather, distracted from my mission, I followed the sounds.

Unfortunately, it led me to Benedictine, the school Jusin taught at. To my dismay, it was a military academy.

The green-uniformed boys were performing drills in an empty parking lot, while an enormous man in a military uniform yelled at them. This flew in the face of church teachings, and I was appalled.

During every mass, there would be a part of the service where you would wish your fellow congregants peace. It was known as the Rite of Peace, and was my favorite part of the service.

"May the peace of the Lord be with you." The priest would intone.

The congregation then replied, "And with your spirit."

Then the priest would say, "Let us offer each other a sign of peace."

This was when people would kiss or hug their neighbors, wishing them peace and goodwill. But how on earth did a catholic school teach students about peace while simultaneously instructing them on how to make war? Like most of the church's teachings, it made zero sense.

I realized I was standing on the sidewalk across the street from the school just staring. If I wanted to be called out as a stalker, I was going about it the right way. I forced my gaze away from the poor boys, and began strolling slowly down the block, keeping my eyes open for Justin.

The school and the church took up an entire city block, so I began circling the red bricked buildings. On the other side from where the boys were being drilled, was the entrance to the church. Two priests exited, and my heart began to pound.

One was in black, while the other was dressed in typical vestments, so I assumed he'd just said mass.

A large Magnolia tree was across the street, and I could see the museum I'd been to last Friday across a small park. There was a line of benches bordering the street, and one of them had a sign indicating it was a bus stop. I decided to watch from there.

I sat down, pulled out my phone, and pretended to be scrolling through it. The two priests strolled down the sidewalk, then crossed the street coming in my direction.

"Oh shit." I mumbled, and without thinking I made the sign of the cross. That was a lifetime habit that would take effort to stop. The closer they got to me, the slower time seemed to pass. It seemed like forever, but finally they walked past me, neither of them sparing me a glance.

I sighed with relief, then noted the time. It was three in the afternoon, and if I guessed correctly, the school day was ending soon. I glanced toward the building to the right of the church, and saw boys in uniform through green tinted windows. They'd just gotten to their feet, and were saluting someone, probably a drill instructor. A bell rang, and I jumped in my seat. A few seconds later the large front door to the building flew open, and chattering boys with backpacks slung over their shoulders poured down the granite steps.

"Where are you, Justin?" I whispered, but no priests exited the building, only students. I'm sure he had other duties, or had to grade papers. All I knew was he wasn't there, and there was no sign of him in any of the windows facing me.

"Mateo?"

I turned at the sound of his voice.

"Justin," I breathed. He stood less than five feet from me.

I licked my lips, willing myself to get to my feet, but I was paralyzed with fear.

"What are you doing here?" He sat next to me on the bench, and a tear slid down the side of his nose. "Why aren't you at the monastery?"

Chapter Six

JUSTIN

My last class was a study hall I supervised on the third floor. While the students studied, I was supposed to be grading papers. Instead, my gaze kept wandering to the window. It was a sunny day, and try as I might to focus on my duties, I couldn't. Several of the boys also had wandering eyes, and I couldn't blame them.

I got up from the desk and strolled over to the windows, and what I saw shocked me.

Mateo, seated on a bench across the street. It had to be him this time, not my imagination. I spun around and smiled at the students.

"Class, it's such a beautiful day. If you promise to be quiet, I'll let you leave now instead of waiting for the bell."

Every open book shut at once, and the boys silently packed up their things and filed out of the classroom, with me right behind them. I was sure I had just broken numerous rules letting the boys out early, but I couldn't help myself. Mateo was here, and obviously, it was to see me. The big question, though, was why?

I tiptoed down the concrete stairs, while the boys' dress shoes sounded like a herd of elephants. When we got to the ground floor, the pupils headed toward their lockers, and I let myself out through a side exit on the other side of the building. Mateo was sitting in view of the administrative offices, and until the bell rang, I couldn't risk being seen by my bosses.

I walked around the building and watched Mateo. His gaze was firmly on the windows of the school, while his hand rubbed his thigh and his brow furrowed. Pressure built behind my eyes, because whatever brought him here had to be important, important enough to risk coming here to where I worked.

The bell rang, and a moment later, I hurried down the sidewalk to where he sat.

"Mateo?"

His brown eyes widened, and I thought he was about to stand, but he licked his lips and just stared at me for a moment. "What are you doing here?" I sat next to him, resisting the urge to take his hand. "Why aren't you at the monastery?"

"I…" Mateo faltered for a moment. "Can we go somewhere else? Someplace we can talk in private?" His dark eyes left mine for a split second and focused on the school. "This isn't a good place for me to say what needs to be said."

"Yeah, sure." I mumbled, and my scalp tingled. Whatever he wanted to tell me must be serious. "Let me grab my belongings from inside, then we can get a drink."

I DIDN'T KNOW the area well yet, so we strolled around the neighborhood until we came upon a cafe in a basement, called Chioca's. It was a small space, more of a bar than a coffeehouse. Its concrete walls were covered in vintage prints and sports paraphernalia. We were the only customers and chose a booth near the rear.

"I'm glad we're in a bar. This conversation requires something stronger than coffee." Mateo smiled uncertainly, and I wanted to take him in my arms and assure him that everything would be okay.

"Welcome to Chioca's, Father." An older waitress grinned. "It's happy hour. A pitcher of beer is only five bucks."

"Sounds good to me. Mateo?"

He nodded, and the waitress sauntered back to the bar and filled a pitcher. We said nothing while waiting for the beer. Once she set the pitcher and mugs on the table, I waited for Mateo to begin.

He picked up a mug and filled it, and I noticed his fingers trembling. He placed the mug in front of me, then filled his own. After taking a sip of beer, he steepled his fingers under his chin and sighed. "There's no easy way to tell you this."

Dizziness shimmered through me. "Sometimes it's best just to spit it out."

Mateo's lips twisted, then he downed half the contents of his mug. "I've left the church."

My head jerked back. "Wait, what?"

"I can no longer be a priest, because…" Mateo drummed his fingers on the table. "… I don't believe any more. And I thank you for my freedom."

"Me?" I froze.

"Yes. When we were together at the monastery, it was

torture." Mateo shook his head, then drained the rest of his beer and refilled the mug. "Because I felt so happy, yet miserable at the same time. I don't want to feel that way ever again, and the only way that will happen is to abandon my former beliefs. If there is a God, they'd want us to be loved, to be happy, and to thrive. Staying with the church prevents all of that."

I opened my mouth to speak, but nothing came out.

"Our entire relationship is twisted by our religious beliefs, Justin. Think about it. When we first met, you deluded yourself into believing that having sex with me would cure you of your attraction to men." Mateo's gaze dropped to the table. "I guarantee it didn't work, right?"

My pulse raced, and instead of answering him, I simply nodded.

"I can't read your mind, Justin, but I can tell you of my experience. Becoming a priest was a decision made out of fear. After being told my entire life I'd go to hell if I acted on my natural desires, I joined the clergy to stay in God's good graces." Mateo said, then he reached across the table, his hand hovering over mine for a moment before returning it to his lap. "I'm not going to hell, if that place even exists. You know why?"

I shook my head.

"Because I've already been there, and now I'm free. No more living in fear of eternal damnation, and following man-made rules about how to conduct my life. I don't need a Pope telling me I'm not worthy if I eat meat on Fridays, or that my feelings for another man are sinful. And I owe it all to you." His somber face split with a smile. "Are you going to say anything? Because I'm feeling self-conscious now."

I studied his features, carefully choosing my words. "Mateo, this is an awful lot to process."

His smile flattened.

"I wouldn't be a priest if it weren't for you, and now you've walked away from it all." I sighed, then picked up my mug and drank the contents down. "My beliefs haven't changed."

Mateo opened his mouth, but I held up my hand for silence. "I went to confession after our last encounter. After-ward, I felt cleansed of my sins. It's a ritual that reassures me and brings me closer to God. When men become priests, it's like becoming royalty. You are held to a higher standard, and the clergy lead people through both example and compas-sion. When I took my vows, I made a promise to God, and to my community."

The door to the bar flew open, and a group of teenagers strolled in. The girls wore the uniform of Benedictine's sister school, St. Gertrude, and the boys were in their military uniforms. They eyed me in my clerical clothing, then sat on the opposite side of the room.

"Did you see the way those kids looked at you?" Mateo lifted a brow. "They're terrified of you, a priest, and for what you represent."

"A teacher who wants them to behave, worship God, and to do their homework?" Where the hell was Mateo taking this conversation? And did I want to examine my beliefs, instead of celebrating our... shit. There was no future for us. No matter how happy I was to see Mateo, and to be in his arms again, it wasn't meant to be.

"You are a representation of God to those kids." He nodded in their direction, where the middle-aged waitress was taking their orders. "You are also a symbol of good and evil, though you are nothing more than a simple man. When they see you, they consciously and unconsciously worry about their behavior, and it's not healthy since Catholicism is based on outdated rules made thousands of years ago. For example, what if that pretty blonde over there has sex with that boy holding her hand. That's one sin in the can. If they used birth control, there's another. Or worse, what if their birth control fails? And what happens if her health is in danger from the pregnancy and she has an abortion? That's a biggie. But, according to the church, all she has to do is go to confession, and be magically absolved of those sins with a few choice words from you."

"But…"

"Don't tell me I don't understand how it all works. Remember, I've walked in your shoes. It's all a lie, and deep down, Justin, you know it." Mateo shook his head, reached into his pocket, and threw a few bills on the table. "I should never have come to see you. You have my apology."

Without thinking, I grabbed his wrist. "Wait."

"For what? I don't think…"

"Give me time to think about what you've said. It's overwhelming. Let me at least walk you back to where you're staying."

Mateo sighed. "Sure. Let's get out of here."

<hr>

NEITHER OF US spoke on our stroll through the Museum District. I was frightened of saying or doing the wrong thing, and Mateo? I couldn't read his mind, but I could see his determination. He appeared both worn down and serene. And, as usual, the sight of Mateo made my blood boil with desire. But I sensed I couldn't tell him that, and couldn't share with him my feelings. For the first time since I'd met this enigmatic man, I was at a loss for what to say or do.

We turned on to Hanover Avenue, and Mateo pointed up ahead. "My Airbnb is in that brick building, with the balcony on the second floor."

I hesitated, and Mateo stopped in his tracks. "Maybe you shouldn't come all the way with me."

I knew why he said it, but I placed a hand on the small of his back and urged him forward. Yes, every fiber of my being wanted to feel his skin burning next to mine. God would forgive me, even if I couldn't forgive myself.

We walked up the brick steps, then Mateo slid a key into the wooden door. "It's not much, just a small one-bedroom apartment. I have it for the next few weeks, enough time to figure out my future. Will I stay here, or move back to El Salvador?"

The door opened, and he entered first. We climbed a narrow flight of stairs, then he unlocked another door and turned to me. "Justin, why don't you go home and think about everything I said. It's not like I'm forcing you to quit the church. All I've done is give you something to think about."

My stomach flipped, and reality sank in. Mateo didn't want me, and was sending me on my way. Then why the hell did he come to Richmond? He could have written a letter, gotten in touch with me in some other way. This made little sense.

"Mateo," I opened my arms, and he drew back.

"Justin, I refuse to make love with you, because you'll feel guilty, and then you'll do what countless other priests have done for centuries." Mateo's eyes snapped shut for a moment, then he opened them and stared directly into mine. "Go to confession, believing you've sinned, and afterwards think God has forgiven you." Mateo placed his hands on my chest and pushed me backwards into the hallway. "I refuse to play any part in your self-delusions."

The door shut in my face.

Chapter Seven

JUSTIN

I stared at the closed door, then leaned against the wall and shut my eyes. An unbidden image filled my head. It was Father Manny, clad only in a flimsy white towel in the sauna, his face leering at me through the steam.

"What goes on in the sauna stays in the sauna, if you know what I mean."

Was that how I'd live the rest of my days? Cruising for sex in steam rooms, then rushing off to confession to make myself feel better?

"No." I whispered, then slowly trudged down the stairs. When I was out on the sidewalk I turned in the direction of my apartment, which was only a few blocks away. Maybe Mateo was right, but what if he was wrong? What if God really existed, and the church was right? Damn it, my entire life had been focused on the church. Even my mother, the washed-up drunk actress, truly believed with all her heart. Otherwise she would have granted my father a divorce years ago. Jesus, my parents were miserable all because of the damned church. How would she react if I were to admit Mateo was right?

"Oh shit." I suddenly couldn't move, and a teenage girl ran into me on the sidewalk. "Oh, sorry." I mumbled, then forced my feet to move. Car horns beeped from a distance, and I saw the Carytown district up ahead. It was all shops, coffee houses, and bars. A drink would be perfect right now, because more than anything I didn't want to think about what had happened with Mateo, or the doubts now worming their way through my soul.

"ANOTHER SHOT, PADRE?"

I nodded, and the bartender pulled the bottle of tequila off the shelf and poured it. Of course, I'd ended up at a gay bar named Babe's, though it was filled with more lesbians than gay guys. If any of my fellow priests saw me in here, there would be hell to pay.

"There is no hell." I mumbled, then tossed the shot back, and bit into a wedge of lime. I hated the taste of tequila, but it was the most efficient booze for forgetting. Though I was doing precious little of that. Three shots in, and it only made me think about Mateo, and my beliefs, more.

I remembered how proud Mom was when I took the vows. Her entire life she'd pushed me into the church's embrace, and I knew if I quit, she'd be destroyed. But I had to admit, Mateo made several good points. And even when we first met, I'd told him I thought the church was wrong about divorce. Now, I thought the church was wrong about many other things.

It was perfectly normal to be gay, according to church

teachings. But, you weren't allowed to act on it, since sex outside of the bonds of marriage was a massive sin. So why on earth didn't the church allow same-sex marriage? Oh yeah, because of the bible, written centuries ago by superstitious men.

Birth control was another biggie I didn't understand. The church celebrated heterosexual love, but sex was only for procreation, so naturally, birth control was a sin.

"If it's human nature, the church is against it." I grumbled.

"What's that?" Asked the bartender, a middle-aged woman wearing a baseball cap with the pride flag on it.

"Sorry, just thinking aloud." I replied, and the woman pointed at the empty shot glass in front of me. I nodded my head, and she poured another one.

"We don't get a lot of your kind here." She placed the tiny glass in front of me.

"My kind?"

"You know, priests." She smiled, curiosity evident on her face.

"I'm having one of those days." I muttered, and realized my words were slurring. "Are you catholic?"

She lifted an eyebrow. "Not anymore."

I sighed audibly, and the woman reached over and patted my hand. "It can't be that bad, whatever it is."

"I'm losing my faith. Actually, it's never been that strong. I became a priest for all the wrong reasons, and now I'm making a huge decision." I sighed again. "I can't fuck this up."

The bartender's hand flew to her chest.

"Would you mind leaving me alone for a while?" I asked,

and this time my words definitely slurred. "I don't want to talk about it."

AFTER FINISHING MY DRINKS, I settled up with the bartender and left. It was dark now, and I stumbled back in the direction I came from. A few short minutes later I was staring up at Mateo's apartment. According to my phone it was only ten in the evening, but his lights were off.

"Damn it, Mateo. Where are you?"

"Are you drunk?"

I glanced up, surprised. Mateo was on the balcony, his face illuminated by the moon. "Maybe."

"Stay there." He ordered, and seconds later I heard feet racing down the steps. The front door of the building flew open. "Come here."

He opened his arms, and when I stepped up to him, he wrapped them around me. "I'm so sorry, Justin. I've been worried sick about you. You didn't deserve to…"

"You're right about everything, Mateo." A sob escaped, and his arms tightened around me. "I don't know what to do."

"C'mon, let's go upstairs, and I'll put on a pot of coffee."

THERE WERE two lawn chairs on the balcony, with a tiny green plastic table in between them. Mateo placed a lit candle on it, along with a steaming cup of joe.

"Take off your jacket, and your collar, too." Mateo ordered. I stood up, swaying on my feet. The jacket came off easily, but the collar was too much for my drunk fingers to handle. "Here. I've got that." Moments later the starched white collar came off, and Mateo strolled back into the apartment. I sat again, rubbing my neck where the collar had chafed my skin.

"Where'd you go?" Mateo sat next to me and picked up his cup.

"I ended up at a place called Babe's." I tried to smile, but it didn't work. "A gay bar. I'd never been to one before."

"Drink your coffee." Mateo sighed, and we sat in silence for a few moments. "Are you going to be okay? Because I know when I…"

"How am I going to tell my mother? And what about my job?" I put my face in my hands, and realized I'd been crying. "My entire life is centered around the church. Hell, Mom was just on the Catholic channel a few weeks ago, celebrating her son, the new priest."

Mateo rubbed between my shoulders. "Are you living your life, or your mother's?"

"Mine, I'm just terrified."

"It's scary realizing everything you ever thought to be true is one big lie." Mateo said, and when I removed my face from my hands he was smiling. "But after you deal with that terrible fact, you feel freer, lighter, actually."

"I still believe in God." I said, and swiped at my eyes with the back of my hand. "It's the church, and the crazy rules they want us to live under."

"I don't believe in God, personally. Somehow that belief vanished with everything else, but it's okay to believe whatever you want, Justin. I just want you to be happy." Mateo said, and his hand moved from between my shoulders up to the back of my head. His fingers pushed up into my hair, and shivers coursed down my spine.

This made me happy. Sitting with Mateo in the light of a candle and the moon. No pressure, no feeling like I would burn in hell for feeling affection for this amazing man.

"Mateo?"

"Yes?"

"I can't go back to the school tomorrow."

I turned and met his dark eyes with mine. "I can't keep teaching those kids about…"

"Let's go to bed, Justin. You can start your new life in the morning."

"Mateo?" My heart pounded, because I was about to say something I never had before.

"Yes?"

"I think I love you." Mateo's hand froze in my hair, then his fingers began to stroke me again.

"Yeah." Mateo whispered, and I sat up straight. His hand dropped to my shoulder. "Justin?"

"Yes?"

"I know I love you."

Epilogue

MATEO- ONE YEAR LATER

"I know this isn't much of a honeymoon, but…"

"Hey, I'm loving this." Justin grinned, and slugged back the rest of his beer. I grabbed one out of the cooler, opened it, and handed it to him. We were on a large rock in the center of the James River, soaking up the sun. Neither of us made much money, so after we were married by a justice of the peace at the courthouse downtown, we were taking a week off from both our jobs.

"I got a letter from Mom yesterday." Justin adjusted his sunglasses and smiled. "I'm going to hell, bless her heart. There was even a splash or two of red wine on the stationary. She must have switched from Chardonnay."

Every month or so a letter would show up, barely legible. We tried to laugh it off, but I know it hurt Justin. His father, the television producer, was thrilled for us, and had even flown the two of us to Los Angeles for a long weekend. While we were there we'd attempted contact with his mother, but she refused to see us.

"I'm sorry, Justin." I sighed. "She'll come around one day."

He stared at me for a long moment. "No, she won't. Oh, she's going to be on Sister Angelica's show tonight."

"Did she tell you that?" I asked. If she had, that meant she'd been at least partially sober when writing it.

"No, I have a google alert set for Mom's name. Maybe one day she'll…" Justin's voice trailed off, and I stuck my feet in the chilly water.

There was nothing I could say to make his relationship with his Mom better. Luckily, my mother was more approving. We still couldn't afford to visit El Salvador, but I did manage to send her a little cash every month. Currently we were saving money for a trip to see her, and I'd been teaching Justin a little Spanish.

Justin found a job teaching with the Richmond public school system, and I managed a latino grocery store. I could've taught at one of the local universities, but the thought of being paid so little for so much work discouraged me. Personally, I didn't know how Justin stomached it, since he spent a sizable portion of his paycheck on school supplies for his students.

"Guess who I saw this morning at the Y?" Justin grabbed the bottle of sunscreen and started smearing it over his legs.

"Let me guess. Our Lady of The Sauna?" I waggled my eyebrows.

"Yes!" Justin laughed. "And Father Manny hasn't changed a bit. In fact, now that I've left the church he's redoubled his efforts to get me to sleep with him. I'm going to stop going there, and just fork out a little extra cash for another gym."

When Justin woke up the next day after making his decision, he didn't give notice, just wrote the Bishop a letter saying he'd quit. The Bishop responded with that bullshit line that once you are a priest, you're always considered a priest. It was like the fucking mafia, and they wouldn't ever let us go.

"So, are we watching Sister Angelica's show tonight, or do you want to skip being tortured for a change?" His mother popped up on the show every few months. Justin claimed it was to keep her floundering career alive.

"What do you think?"

<hr>

"DID you know Sister Angelica's show is filmed in a garage?" Justin placed a bowl of popcorn between us on the couch as I aimed the remote at the television. Seconds later, the ancient nun's face filled the screen.

"One of my favorite guests is back with us tonight. Please welcome actress Margot Finnegan!"

Justin's mother walked onto the set, and the canned applause sounded almost real. She bowed toward the camera, then took her seat.

"I think she's sober." Justin sighed. "Though she looks kind of bloated."

"So a little bird told me you have important news to tell us about." Sister Angelica beamed at his mother. "But first we'd love to hear about your son, the priest."

His mother's face reddened, then she flashed a brilliant white smile at the camera. "Ah, my loving son is doing well, still teaching the good news to God's flock."

"Wow. That was a whopper." I giggled, but the look on Justin's face silenced me. She wasn't technically lying, since we were both still priests according to the church.

"I will be starring in a Hallmark movie, reprising my role as Sister Marie Constance from the hit TV show Creating Hope." His mother's eyes crinkled, then I noticed they had a pink sheen to them. She wasn't as sober as she was letting on. Why do Catholics drink so much? To dull the pain?

"That's outstanding news, Margot." Sister Angelica said through a crooked smile, and I wondered if the old nun wasn't buzzing on something, too.

Justin switched the television off. We sat in silence for a few moments, then Justin moved the popcorn and laid his head on my shoulder. "I wish Mom would…"

His words faded off, and there was nothing I could say. Justin wanted a normal mother, who loved him for who he actually was. Instead, he had an alcoholic mother who wouldn't speak or see him. And why? Because of her silly, archaic beliefs.

"Why is your Mom so cool about us, and mine isn't?" Justin whispered.

"Love. That's a core teaching of the church, something most Catholics forget about. She wants me to be happy." I kissed the top of his head. "Are you happy, Justin?"

"For the first time in my life, yes. I mean, it sucks having Mom act all strange about me, but living my truth instead of faking it like most people do is worth it." He looked up at me. "Thanks for showing me the truth, Mateo. I love you dearly for that."

Warmth spread through my limbs. "I love you too, Justin."

THANK you for enjoying Mateo and Justin's romance. This story originally began as a simple story about a filthy priest. But, characters can run away from an author, and the story takes on a different flavor. I'm grateful Justin and Mateo fell in love.

About the Author

Luke Jameson is the steamy pen name for bestselling author Ian O. Lewis. He's originally from Richmond, Virginia, but currently lives in Mexico. Follow him on Bookbub, Facebook, or Instagram to stay up to date with him and his work. Oh, and friend him- Ian loves his readers!